CU01507802

Written by: Ash Ericmore

Copyright © 2021 Ash Ericmore

ISBN: 9798361677450

C H A P T E R   1

Pencil moustache. Slicked back hair. Thin face. He was sitting in the park. About thirty metres from the playground. He was wearing one of those oversized beige mackintosh things. He looked like a parody of a paedophile. But he wasn't a parody. He'd been in the papers. About four years back.

Forgotten by everyone now.

Well. Most people.

He was probably only sitting that far away because he had to. Legally. He didn't want to get in any shit while he was sitting there. Plotting. Planning. Fantasizing. He had on glasses. Little round Harry Potter things. Made him look a bit like Hitler. What with the hair. His shoes were clean. Polished. Like the rest of him. He looked like he'd made an effort to scrub up, but didn't actually know what it *meant* to scrub up. That was probably it. He was staying in a bed and breakfast on the seafront. Fucking tourist town and they put the fucker in a halfway house in the middle of it.

Most of their ... clients ... were probably fine. Rehabilitated and such. But not this one. Not Harold Burnley. 'The Burn', they called him. When it went to trial. He got six years with time off for good behaviour because of a technicality. Half of the evidence wasn't able to be submitted. Someone didn't sign something in the right place. Whatever. It happens. The trial hadn't happened around there, either. Up north somewhere. They'd re-located him to the sunny seaside so he didn't get murdered the first night he was out, by some parent. Maybe one of the parents of one of the kids he fiddled. Maybe one worried he'd do it again. Look at him.

Of *course* he was going to do it again.

Christ, he was probably wearing the oversized coat to hide his hard-on. Over the kids. On the swings. According to the reports he hadn't been picky over whether it was boys or girls, as long as they were four to seven. Even now, he was probably trying to pick one. Maybe not to take, but to fantasize about later. Like the playground was a lunchtime menu. He would be licking his lips thinking of the early bird menu—what with it being lunchtime—maybe a set menu. Wondering what he was going to partake in. Probably wondering the best way of wooing a kid these days. It had been a while since he'd practiced. But he was thinking about it. He was drawn to it. *Them.* The kids. Addicted, maybe? It'd been what, five years since he'd preyed on one? Maybe times had changed? His banter would have to change.

His sales pitch.

What would it have been back then? He never said a word during the trial, and his victims didn't say much about the grooming process. They were far too young. Video evidence, too. So they didn't have to appear in court. The old saying though, isn't it? Sweets in a van. Puppies. Kittens. Wanna stroke this? The four year old's would probably still be the same. No idea what they wanted, but how much could it

6

have changed in those years? The others. Seven year olds—they might have been into Tik-Tok now. Youtube. He suddenly looked hungry. Not for food either. He looked like normal people did when they're at a strip club. Or do they call them Gentleman's Clubs these days? Didn't matter. Places to legally get their rocks off. Sex work *is* work, right?

But not Harold. He was in the park. Checking out the smorgasbord of things he wanted to fuck.

Amelia shuddered. She was sitting on the opposite side of the playground to Harold. She was a little closer to the kids than he was, you know, because she *could* be. Watching him. She was wearing a long white coat. Thin fabric thing. No idea where it had come from. Just a purchase on a whim at some point in the past, no doubt. Paris, maybe. It wasn't cold enough to be wearing a big coat. Not like Harold's. She was wearing a floppy hat too. Something she might have worn to Ascot last year. She uncrossed her legs. Stood. Never once taking her eyes from Harold.

She'd been watching him since he'd arrived at the station. He arrived at Birchingate station six hours after he'd been released from Stafford prison. *Six hours*. It was like he'd been ferried there by the prison service. Fuck it. He probably was. That was where she'd gotten the tip-off from, after all. The tip-off that he was going to be there. *In her hometown.*

She started walking down and around the playground, in the general direction of the paedophile. Sat watching. The one no one else had even noticed.

CHAPTER 2

Amelia approached the bench Harold was sitting on from the front. This bit was always a little hit or miss. Nervous, paedophiles tended to be. You know, in case someone knew what they were up to.

She turned and sat at the other end of the bench from him. She could feel him glancing to her. Worried that she was going to challenge him. She just let her stare sit on the playground, the kids. "Nice day," she said. There was no one else there. He would know she was talking to him. This was the crunch time, really. One of two things would happen. One, he would get up and walk away. Rumbled. Afraid. Flee. Two, he'd be cocky. Not willing to even consider that she might know who he was.

Honestly, this guy looked like a fucking paedo. The chance of him being in the second category was considerably unlikely.

She still didn't look at him.

"Yes," he whispered.

She felt like he was somewhere between the two. He was nervous about being called out, but he was too involved to tear his eyes from the children. Sexy little things.

It made Amelia want to vomit first, then tear his cock off and feed it to him. Or vice versa. It didn't really matter. She looked from the children playing, to the *man*. Man. The word stuck in her throat. "I like to watch the children playing. You?" She saw him flinch. Caught out. He didn't respond. She could see the *flee* rising in him, but still he couldn't take his eyes from them. Lust. "None of them are mine," she continued. "I just like to … watch." She left the word on the end to hang. Noosed. She could see him twitch. The excitement. It was there. That of a kindred spirit. It made her want to shudder, but she swallowed it back. Not happening. Not now. Not now she was so close.

"I have a plaything at my house. Would you be interested?"

What? It had worked before.

Harold raised the side of his mouth. Like he was going to smile and then his body fought back. Don't smile, it was saying. It's a fucking trap.

Of course it was a fucking trap. But he couldn't help himself. Could he?

"You can watch me fuck him if you like. Or join in. I would prefer it that way." She dropped her voice to a whisper. "If you … joined in."

Still no response. Harold. Staring at the children. Unflinching. Unmoving. Blinking too much.

"Or have I got it wrong? Maybe I shouldn't have spoken. You just … looked like me." Amelia stood. She didn't take her eyes from him. Burning into him. He still hadn't torn his eyes from the children. He had to be able to see her in his peripheral. But he wasn't going to admit it. *That he wanted it.* There was an internal struggle going on. The rational—what laughable rational thought a man like that could have—telling him to get up and walk away. Run. She was a copper. She was a narc. One of those bashers who trap people like … Harold. Then there was the other half of him. The hearted half. The half that was full of desire. Wont. Need. Lust. The part of him that made his cock wet. It was telling him to follow her. Be led to the child, to the fuck. To the watch. Her.

He glanced at her.

She was beautiful. Twenties. Tight clothes. Probably had the firm body of a teenager under the clothing. Two for the price of one.

But she was turning. Leaving. One last glance back to him. His eyes flickered from her body to her sunglasses. He wanted to see her eyes. But he couldn't.

Then he had to make the choice.

He knew.

She knew he knew. That was the hook. Amelia started walking across towards the park edge. Where she'd parked her car. That was it. She wasn't to look back again. He had his chance. Take it. *Take it.*

The wind rose. Cut through the park. The playground was in the valley that ran through the centre of the park, a slow slope on either side of it. Amelia wrapped her arms around her coat. She watched the guy with a doggo in the distance. Throwing a ball. Run. Chase. Return. She walked to the path and followed that to the road. Her car. Red. Audi. High performance, of course. But it had a lot of boot space, too. She dug in her pocket, rested her hand on the fob. As she got close to the car it unlocked itself.

It wasn't until she started to round the car to the driver's door did she look. Look to see if Harold 'The Burn' Burnley had taken the bait.

Of course he had.

C H A P T E R   3

Shifty looking cunt, he was, as he followed her to the car. Had to be. Hitler looking motherfucker wandering along behind a girl half his age. She stopped. Stared at him. He was standing ten feet from the car. Neither of them smiled. There was no acknowledgement between them. He just raised his eyebrows and continued. He walked to the car and got in.

Amelia waited until he closed the door, before she got in next to him. Closed her door. "Amelia," she said. She didn't look at him. She wasn't about to shake his hand either.

"Harry."

Harry. So innocent. So blameless. Harry. You know. From down the pub. Straight up geezer. Works down the bins. Harold. Paedophile. Hangs around in parks. Time off for good behaviour.

She pushed the ignition. Started the car. Pulled out onto the road. "I don't live far," she said. She could smell him. Now they were in the car. In the enclosed space. He smelt like cough drops. Medicinal. Clean. Too clean. Like he'd washed something off himself too many times. Scrubbed 'til the skin was raw. Itchy. Flaky. Then scrubbed some more. She dropped the window down an inch.

"Nice motor," he said.

Great. Small talk.

"I always wanted a fast car," he said, smiling.

Amelia hadn't looked at him. But she knew he felt safe now. In the car. The woman in the park was for real. There was going to be sex. Young skin. Supple. She could feel his eyes on her. Her legs, bare, now she'd sat with them into the foot well. Her white dress drawn up her body.

"It suits my personality," he continued, talking about the car. "Sweet?"

She glanced. He was holding a small white paper bag towards her. He must have pulled it from the manky coat he was wearing. Free candy. She shook her head. "No, thank you." The words caught in her throat again. Being *nice* to him.

He withdrew the bag. Stuck his fingers in. Rummaged. Took out a fucking red thing. Aniseed or something. Stuck it in his gob. Fingers went in too. Pushing the thing into his mouth. Then the bag went back in the coat. "So how long have you been in the game?"

The game. So open. *Safe spaces.* "A while." Another glance to him. He was watching out the window intently. Making sure he knew where he was, no doubt. It didn't matter. She pulled the car onto the dual carriageway out the town. Out through the villages. She knew where all the speed cameras were. She knew all the low traffic routes. She'd lived around Birchingate her whole life—bar the four years at University—and knew how to get around. No trouble.

He seemed impressed.

Out to the villages on the outskirts. Beyond that. Another dual carriageway. To a roundabout. Small village ahead, then out to Ashbury. She turned right. Then off a small turning before the dual carriageway became a motorway.

Taking the car onto private land. The gates beyond the turn off opened as she approached, electronics exceeding her comprehension recognising the car or something. And she drove through. Then they closed behind her.

Harold whistled in appreciation. "Nice," he said. He rubbed his open palms down his legs, still covered by the oversized coat. He thought he'd landed on his feet. He was looking forward to what was to come.

Through the trees. Onto the driveway.

"Hellingate House," she said as they broke the tree line and Harold could see the homestead for the first time.

"Holy shit," he whispered. Then, "Do excuse my French."

Amelia nodded. She couldn't care less about how much he said. What he said.

"This pad is amazing."

Amelia smiled to herself. "Indeed."

The house dated back several hundred years. It was the ancestral home. Been in the family since it was built. It dominated the landscape inside the treeline. Couldn't be seen from the roads on any side.

If you didn't know better, the turn off looked nothing more than a layby. The house had three storey's going up. One basement. Originally eleven bedrooms. Some had been converted over the years. It sat in its own estate. Stables, lake, land. Pheasants. All that sort of shit. And money. Amelia didn't know how much money she had. Her father had only just died—a few months back—but her accountant had been flippant when she'd asked what it was all worth, and whether she needed to liquidate; what cash she had available. He'd simply shaken his head and said, *No need to liquidate, Miss. Strange. You have all the money. Like, all of it.* He raised his eyebrows. That seemed to be the end of it. The accountancy was a family run place. It seemed to have been in the employ of the family forever. So she had just taken his word for it.

As the car approached the house, the gravel drive under tire, the front door of the house opened and a man stepped out.

"Who's this?" Harold snatched out the words. A sudden realisation that he was vulnerable.

"That's my new butler. Cousins," she replied. "Don't worry about him."

"New butler," he echoed in a whispered.

Amelia pulled the car to the front of the house and killed the engine. Opened the door. Out. She kept moving. Nothing wrong. Nothing to see here. She had a side-eye on Harold who had yet to disembark. *Come on.* She strode over to Cousins.

"Hello, Madam." He smiled. "Did we have a

good trip?"

Amelia smiled. "Fine. Did you have any luck with finding another case?"

"Yes, Madam."

"Good. Put the details in my study." She glanced back to Harold. Waved him out the car. He seemed to need encouragement. The door opened. Slowly. "And stop calling me Madam," she said to Cousins.

Harold put his foot out onto the drive.

"Yes … Amelia."

She could hear the distain oozing in his words. "Come on then," she called to Harold.

He finally got out.

Cousins went off in the direction of the kitchen and Amelia dropped her coat over the rack at the front door, along with her hat. They'd be gone before she returned, and they'd be brought back to her when she wanted them again. Or she'd find them in the wardrobe in her closet. It was still a mystery how it all worked. She led Harold through the doors at the base of the stairs. Into a short corridor. The place was a like a rabbit warren when you weren't used to it. "Through here," she said. His lust was driving him forward. With each step he was taking she knew that he was becoming more and more uncomfortable.

But he couldn't stop.

"Where are you taking me?" he asked. Barely a whisper.

"Down here," she said, smoothing the white fabric of the slender dress she wore beneath the coat. It looked cocktail-y. A small room at the end corridor. Another door. Only one. Amelia rested her hand on the handle and looked back at Harold. He looked sweatier. It could have been excitement. Could have been nerves. He still wasn't sure if he could trust her.

But the desire pushed his feet. One in front of the other.

She smiled. "Don't look so worried. This *will* be fun." She pushed the door open a little. "Vic," she called. "I'm home." Pushed the door fully open.

Flicked the light on beyond. A set of wooden stairs down. Into the basement. She started on them. Waved Harold forward. "Close the door behind you," she said. "Keeps the noise in." Down. Into the gloom.

Harold hesitated at the top of the stairs.

"Amelia?" came a voice from the basement. "Is that you?" A boy. Maybe eight? Seven? Ten? Hard to tell before their balls had dropped and their voices broke.

It didn't matter to Harold. As soon as the voice came, he was *all in*. Through the door. Closing it slowly. Silently. Like he'd done it a thousand times before. Closing bedroom doors without waking the sleeping children. Didn't want them to be afraid. Not yet. Not while he was at the door. No, fear only comes once he's sitting on the edge of the bed. Watching them. Running his fingers over their smooth flesh. *Smooth as a baby's bum*, so the saying went. No one said that sort of shit anymore. Not except Harold.

Amelia waited at the bottom of the stairs, as Harold came down. They led to the centre of the basement, a room that looked to cover nearly the entirety of Hellingate House. It was like he was gliding. Suddenly in a different place. A different mind-set. At the bottom of the stairs she noted that he'd already opened the front of his coat. His hand in the pocket. Pulled out the white paper bag of shitty sweets. Pushed them into the pocket of his trousers. Coat sliding off the shoulders. Down his back. Into his hands and around. Almost suave. Almost smooth.

If the big reveal hadn't been that he was wearing worn trousers. Shirt with the threads showing. Clothes he was probably wearing when he was sent down.

Fucker.

He looked around the room. Ignoring *the room*. He was looking for the source of the voice. The child. The perfect little child. He leant his head in, towards Amelia, stood there, in a cocktail dress, waiting. "Where is the little fella? Vic, you say."

She could hear the horn rising in him. It made her want to vomit. "Vic," she said. "You can come out now. I'm here. I've brought a friend." The word friend almost didn't come out. Vile cunt of a human being.

"I'm here." The voice came from behind the stairs. The boy giggled. Angelic. Childlike. Playful. Hiding.

Harold turned. He discarded his coat onto the stairs. Suddenly at home. He saw the shape, the shadow, of the boy move in the darkness behind the stairs.

Amelia stepped away from Harold. Over to the space in that side of the room. She turned to face him and the stairs. She could see the boy through the gaps in them. Giggles. Harold paid no attention to her. Nor the room. He was absorbed by the boy. The free fuck. On a platter. Given by this woman of great generosity.

The boy scurried away, hidden by the shadows

under there.

Harold pulled that grotty fucking bag from his pocket. Pushed it forwards. Towards where the boy had been. "Would you like a sweet?" he asked. Hunched himself down. Tried to make himself smaller. Less intimidating. He'd all but forgotten about Amelia now, as she watched. Waited patiently for Vic to stop playing with him.

Harold moved around the stairs. He was going to give chase. Find the boy. "Come on now," he was saying. Quietly. Trying to be sweet. A favourite uncle, maybe. Following around into the darkness.

The room was around the stairs, cavernous on all sides. You could chase Vic for hours and never catch him. It was done out in something of a man-cave, the basement had been her father's room for many years. A bar in the corner. Pool table. Blue baize one. Rack of cues. Big screen TV. A couple of sofas. Vic liked it down there. He'd taken to using it as his little nook. For the most part. When he wasn't out with her.

Amelia shook her head. She hadn't asked Cousins to call Owl and book Matthew for the night. Fuck it. It was probably going to be too late by the time this was all done.

Vic appeared from the left of the stairs. He was naked. He looked across the front of them. Leaning forward to see if Harold was still following him around. "Come and find me," he called. He looked at Amelia. Wink.

It was more than a little odd to see the voice of a

small child come from the body of a man. *Man*. She used the term loosely. She didn't think he'd ever been a man. Not a real one. But whatever, that was what he looked like now. Probably early thirties. Some years younger than Harold. Generously sculpted. He was learning what looked right in a body. Cock was still too big. He wouldn't listen when it came to that. What man did? There she went again, referring to him as a *man*.

Vic slipped over to the bar in the corner while Harold was out of sight behind the stairs. He grinned at Amelia, sliding down behind and hiding. It was all a game. It always was until someone got hurt.

Harold reappeared to the left of the stairs. He looked a little put out. Finished with the game now. He wanted his prize. His *pretty* for playing. A trophy. And he still had that fucking bag in his hand. He looked at Amelia. There was something behind his eyes. Like he was beginning to think this was all a joke. Some big setup. But he hadn't done anything wrong. Not now. He hadn't even seen a child. So he wasn't breaking the conditions of his parole.

Amelia met his eyes with hers and guided him to the bar. Looked down. Indicated where the child was hiding.

Harold nodded. Understanding. "I've got you now," he said. Giggle. Mimicking the child-laugh. "I'm coming to get you." He crept across the carpeted floor. It still hadn't occurred to him that this kid was hanging out in a man-cave. Whatever.

He got to the bar.

Amelia slipped around behind him. She probably wasn't going to need to intervene. Not this time.

Harold placed that fucking bag down on the bar and took a deep breath. The absolute fucker was really enjoying this.

Amelia was going to enjoy *this*. Harold peered behind the bar, as she watched. He made this weird noise, like there were words but there was no way they were fucking well coming out. Vic stood.

His skin was blackened red. Hair pure, like a centaur. His form, rippling grotesque, huge mounds of gristle under the charred burnt skin of a demon. Horns, short. Tail, long. Cock was way larger than it was before. He hadn't been birthed, his body had sculpted in a forge. "Hello Uncle Harold," he said. Still had the voice of a child. He grinned. "I want to play now." He dug his hand into that fucking bag and pulled out a hard sweet. Fucking cough drop. Whatever. Popped it in his mouth. "Mmm."

Harold backed away. He didn't know what to make of the demon. Understandably. Made some noised like "Wh" and "Wo" but nothing that was coherent.

"It's just a game," Vic continued. "But it'll be our little secret, yes?"

Dark yellow piss ran from the bottom of Harold's trousers.

Vic looked down at it. "You smell dehydrated." Looked back up. Smiled. He stepped away from the bar. Towards Harold. "Do you want to touch it?" he asked. "It won't hurt."

Harold shook his head. "I-I don't understand."

"It's okay. It's perfectly natural. *We all do it.*" He looked at Amelia. "Did you want some?"

Amelia shook her head. "Have a party." She strode past the two of them to the bar, and slipped in behind, now that Vic had vacated the spot. Pulled out a bottle of vodka and started to mix a Mosco Mule.

Vic turned his attention to Harold. He spat the cough sweet out at Harold's feet. "I don't like aniseed."

Harold backed up. His arse butted up against the pool table. He let out a little squeak. Confused. Afraid. "What?" he managed to mutter.

"You'll enjoy it," Vic said.

Amelia sipped the Mule. Mm. Nice. Leant herself down on the bar. Like she was at some strip show. The Chippendales or whatever they were called. Elbows down. Smile. Cheeky one. The sort of smile that got a girl laid.

Vic placed his massive hand on the pervert's shoulder. Harold's crinkled five year old suit crumpling under the sheer weight of the demons hand. He was burbling nothings. *This isn't possible.* And, *It can't be real.*

But it was.

C H A P T E R 5

Vic turned Harold to face away from him, with Harold left facing the pool table, the demon pushed up behind him, like he was going to teach him how to bowl. Then Vic took a hand full of Harold's hair and slammed his face down onto the flat of the pool table. Pretty fucking hard too. Harold let out a noise like two bumpers kissing each other as an old fool failed to park correctly.

Vic brought his head up. Odd noises coming from the mouth. Dazed. Teeth shattered as they collided with the table. Lips split. Nose pissing blood. He drooled and dribbled red goop as Vic ran the charred, stretched flesh of his hand under Harold's throat. Sensual. Sexual. Caressing him. Pushing the blood around as it ran freely down the pale prison tanned skin of the predator. "I want you," Vic whispered. He leant Harold's head down to the table again. Bending him over it. "I want you, like you wanted them."

"No," Harold said. Weeped. "Fucking hell."

"That's correct," Vic continued. "*Fucking* hell."

He took the back of Harold's trousers in his grip and tore them from him. Holding his head onto the table. Gentle, so as not to hurt him further. Keep him awake. Alive. Conscious. *Aware*. The garment ripped from him. The belt tearing under the violent *yank*. The trousers all but disintegrating. Tatty white pants underneath. Skid marked. Dirty fucking cunt.

Amelia looked from the show to the Mule. Tasty. Back again.

Vic pulled the paedo's pants from his lily white arse. His own cock was raging hard at command of the demon. He turned. Pushed the tip of it to Harold's arsehole. Teased it around the cheeks. He leant forward. Over him. Closer to his head. So he could whisper. Sensually.

"I'm going in dry," he said.

Harold was crying now. Unable to comprehend the monster. The situation. Everything had been coming up Harold until about five minutes ago. Now he was bleeding. Hurt. And it looked like *everything was coming in Harold*, now.

Vic leant forward. Cock the size of a horse's. He pushed it in between the cheeks of Harold. To his virgin pucker. In. Slowly. Sexy, like. "You like it like that, don't you?" In further.

Harold screamed out.

Vic looked back over his shoulder to Amelia. Sly nod and wink. Back to it. In further. Not in halfway and he could feel the heat of Harold's intestines as his cock broke through into his lower gut. Out the colon. "It'll only hurt for a minute," he whispered. He pulled Harold up to stand in front of him. Still connected. Driving Vic deeper inside the vile human being. He reached around and cupped the man's shrivelled cock and balls, so tightly up in his body he could barely feel them. "You'll grow to like it," he said. "I promise. The more you do it, the more fun it becomes." Vic clenched his arse up, the massive stretch of muscles pushing his cock deeper inside Harold. Tearing him. Bursting him open inside.

Blood dribbled and drooled through the hole of Harold's arse, plugged tightly by the girth of Vic. Then Vic started to thrust. Push himself in, out, slowly. Fucking the cunt. Fucking him slowly. Like Harold should enjoy it. Like he'd grow to. "You know what they do to people like you in Hell?" he whispered, quiet. Pillow talk. Grunting lightly, as he began to enjoy it.

Harold's head was lolling about. He was still awake, but he didn't seem to have any control over his body anymore.

Vic's grunting became louder. He was going to cum. Harder into Harold. Faster.

Deeper.

Suddenly Vic tensed, ejaculating deep, somewhere inside Harold. Pulling the small, pathetic man in close to a hug. A single snap as one of Harold's bones gave under the pressure. Arm, leg? Who knew?

Harold let out a cry. Loud. Hard.

Vic let go of him, pushing him forward again, onto the pool table to slump forward, arse in the air. His cock coming out. The pressure of all of Harold's insides being blended together by the demon cock, blended together with the demon's seed, it blew. Like a back firing toilet. Shit. Cum. Blood. Bits of intestine. It all fired out of Harold's arse like a potato gun.

"I hope you're going to clean that up," Amelia said.

Vic looked down at Harold. He was shuddering lightly, twitching perhaps a better word. He dipped his finger into the gaping hole that used to be Harold's tight arsehole. Smelt it. Tasted it. A blood-cum slurpie. "Mmm." He savoured the flavour. "You know me. Of course I will." He slapped Harold on the back. "And how are you doing champ?"

Harold didn't respond.

"Dead?" Amelia asked.

Vic leant down, getting his head level with Harold's broken one, on the pool table. "It appears so."

Amelia nodded. "Then he's in a better place." She stepped away from the bar, taking the Moscow Mule with her. "Don't let the place smell up, will you?"

Vic had already positioned himself on his knees on the pool table over the corpse.

"And don't play with your food."

CHAPTER 6

As luck would have it, Owl Escorts still had Matthew available when she'd gotten hold of Cousins, after leaving Vic to clean up. He'd eat a lot of Harold and get rid of the rest somehow. She really didn't bother with the logistics of what Vic got up to. Not after the soul was taxi'd off to Hell.

She sat at the desk in her office looking at the file that Cousins had left for her. It was a man who beat women. Men. Boys. *A* boy, mostly. His son. *Step-son*, she corrected herself. The file had been sent through by one of her friendlies down at the Crown Prosecution Service. Aaron Rogers his name was. Right piece of shit by all accounts. Still, she never took the CPS's word for it. She'd do her own due diligence—

The doorbell of the house rung elsewhere.

—just to be sure he was the piece of shit that it was claimed. Before she did her thing. Her and Vic. It was a funny story how they got together. But the relationship worked. She might deal with this one on her own though. She liked to keep her hand in.

A rap at the door to her office.

"Come," she called. Gentle. It could only be Cousins. Vic rarely left the basement when he was in the house. And if he did, she was sure he wouldn't knock. Too oafish for that. Too … blokey.

Cousins pushed the door open. "Mr. Matthew

from the Owl Agency is here to visit with you, Madam."

That was right. *Agency*. Not *Escorts*.

"I'll be right there," she said, Cousins leaving her to her business. He didn't really know what went on there. Too new. He knew that Vic lived in the basement. But Vic had never let on he was a demon in front of Cousins. Professional courtesy. He didn't know what went on with the files. Cases. Not yet, anyway. She'd bring him into the fold once she was settled with him. She looked at the picture of Rogers. He looked like anyone else on the street. Could have been anyone else. Had a job. Married. More than once. She closed the file.

That was for later.

She went out to the hallway and across to the library. It was where Cousins would leave anyone that came to the house. Not that they had much in the way of visitors. That went with the family business. She opened the door and Matthew was sitting in one of the reading chairs looking at his phone.

There were literally thousands of books in there, ranging from Charlotte Brontë (fiction) to Occult Rituals (factual), from Jack and Jill (fiction) to Clive Barker (undecided), and Matthew was on his phone. Probably playing some flash game collecting fruits or something. But then he wasn't there for his brains was he?

He looked up and stood immediately, slipping his phone into his pocket. Wearing a sharp suit. He had a fine body under there. She'd had a few of the lads from the agency, but Matthew was her favourite of the moment. He was pliable. Flexible.

Accommodating.

———

Matthew was face down in the pillows. Hands tied behind his back. Amelia had a strap-on firmly up his arse, lubed well, listening to him bite the pillow as she stroked in and out. The belts of the thing had a handy-dandy placed vibe that was pulsing against her. Just in the right place. "Come on," she barked.

She wasn't talking to him. She was talking to herself.

She'd gotten Matthew up there to her bedroom, then gotten him *up there*, before she realised how much *Vic* was rubbing off on her. Sticking it up his arse like that. And some of her heat for it was gone, too. It wasn't like it was her first time doing it, either. That was why she liked Matthew so much. *He* was quite happy to participate in this too.

Naked, she pinched her nipples, trying to get a rise. One that seemed a little lost on her at that moment. *Damn it*, she'd paid for this ride, and she was going to use it one way … or another.

They were in one of the other bedrooms of the house—not her master (or should that be mistress) room—but the one she regularly used for fucking someone. The boys from the agency were easiest, but she did on occasion bring home a stray. Someone that might be a little … rougher. Anyway. The room was done out white. Very virginal. The soon to be stained sheets, white. Wardrobe, white. Mirror. Walls. Ceiling. Amelia found her eyes wandering the room. *Christ*, she must have been off her game. Her eyes fell on the mirror.

Antique.

Free standing thing. Been in the family probably longer than she'd been alive. She was facing the wall (with Matthew betwixt her and it), and in the mirror she could see the doorway. She'd closed it when the two of them had entered, before they'd disrobed. It was open now. In the shadows she could see Vic. He was in human form. Young male. Slightly different to the one that was in the basement earlier. He hadn't seemed to get the hang of taking the same form each time. Particularly without the use of a reflective surface. He was awash with Harold's blood. Blackening as it stuck to his face. On his chin. Chest. Hands. The hand that stroked his cock (still too large), bloody. Cold. Sticky. Getting it on his flesh, his foreskin (Yeah, foreskin. No short cuts in Hell, apparently).

She felt the burn of heat as it sparked in her cunt. The demon watching. Tickling her. She pulled out of Matthew. He let out a little grunt. Like the little guy might be enjoying it. She pulled open the Velcro on the strap on, dragging it off. Tossing it to the side. "Fuck me," she whispered.

Matthew did as instructed. He turned on the bed. Already hard. Hard from her fucking him. Always willing. She immediately turned and slid up his body, her back to him, flat on the bed, and straddled his cock. Big enough. On. Reverse cowgirl. Watching the demon stroke himself. Matthew reaching around her body. Pinching her tits with his thumb, forefinger. She reached down. Helped herself along. The only sound in the room was the sound of the vibe in the strap on, playing to itself. She made eye contact with Vic.

He smiled. Stroked faster.

He didn't always watch. But she liked it when he did. It wasn't done to fuck a demon. Not in her position. But she wanted it.

Him.

C H A P T E R   7

Amelia had instructed Cousins to bring the car round. One of the *cheaper* ones. She didn't want to stick out today. She then went to the basement.

"Who is he?" Vic asked.

"You assume a *he?*" she retorted.

"Isn't it always?"

It wasn't. Just mostly. "Aaron Rogers," she continued. Ignoring his belligerence. "Beating up on the weak."

"Seems simple enough. Where?"

"In the city." Ashbury. A few miles up the road. "Shouldn't take more than a couple of days."

"You need … help?" He was naked. He was always naked when he was in the basement. He glanced to his cock. Winked.

Amelia sighed. "You never change, do you?" She smiled. "No. I can manage. I'll just keep an eye on him. If it turns out he needs processing and I get an opportunity, I'll be on it. If not, I know where to find you." She looked over to the pool table. No traces of Harold. "Well done with the clean up."

He licked his lips. "You're welcome." Wink.

She turned away. Stopped to say something about him watching her fuck. Decided against it. Kept walking.

To the front door.

Cousins was holding it open. "Will your friend not be joining you?" he asked on her approach.

"Not this time. I shan't be gone more than one night I don't expect." She looked out to the Mondeo in the drive. Idling. "Good choice," she said. "I'd leave him to his own devices."

"As you wish, Madam."

She nodded. Down to the car. There was an overnight bag in the boot.

Gates opened as she approached, out onto the dual carriageway. The car was more *normal* than some of her others. Still pretty good on performance though. She'd be in the city in half an hour. She had Rogers file in her bag. She was going to stay at a decent hotel. Drop in there first. Check in. Change into something less … lady of the manor … and then onto the case.

———

Amelia sat in the Mondeo. On the street. The other side of the road from the Rogers house. It's not like they would be expecting anyone to be out there. Not like they were the Sopranos and would be watching for the FBI. But there was a young dude, maybe sixteen, down the street on the corner. She could barely make out his face, but she was sure he wasn't in the file. She stuffed a Gregg's sausage roll in her mouth. Bobbed her head from side to side as she chewed. She managed to switch persona pretty well these days. She brushed the crumbs from her Simpsons t-shirt, onto her jeans and then shuffled, making them fall onto the seat. Someone would clean it up. Later. Okay, she didn't lose the other persona—the lady of the manor—quite as much as she thought she did, but she did okay. She smiled to herself. Glanced to the radio in the car. Probably should be listening to something.

Then the front door of the Rogers house opened.

Damon. The stepson. He was wearing a hoodie. Had the hood up. But she was sure it was him. He slammed the front door and went out to the path. Down towards the corner. He didn't even glance in her direction.

The front door opened again. Aaron. Came out wearing a vest. Wife-beater type. Stained. It looked like someone had pissed on it. He stormed to the gate at the front of the house and stared down the road after Damon. Watching. He looked royally fucked. He watched Damon as he met with the other lad on the corner, the two of them walking off together. It looked like there was some silent greeting between them. Hoods up. Heads down. Skulking.

Amelia turned back to Aaron. He was staring at her. She didn't look away. Perfectly innocently. Sitting there eating a sausage roll. Bite. Chew. Eye contact. It was a bit shit that he'd made her. And he was now probably weighing up his chances. Thinking about hitting on her.

He should not. His chances were not good.

But don't let on, she thought to herself. A twat like him would forget her soon enough. He nodded. One of those nods you'd make in a club to some bird you made eye contact with across the bar. The *I-know-you-see-me-I-see-you-too-and-we-gonna-fuck* look. She took another sausagey bite. Crumbs on the chin. Didn't return the nod. Just stared him down.

He shrugged. Turned back into the house.

Amelia wondered if that ever worked. Seeing some woman on the side of the road and trying to pick her up. Like, *right there*. What a pratt.

She managed to wedge the remainder of the sausage roll in her mouth and started to chew, breathing through her nose. Fucking hell. Too much. This wasn't how she planned on dying. Smiled internally, because actually smiling with a sausage roll jamming up your gob was near on impossible. She started the engine and moved the car. Down the street to where she could still see the gate of the house. Where she could wait for him to leave.

CHAPTER 8

It was the middle of the afternoon. Aaron Rogers finally left the house. He was now wearing some sort of chino things. Button down shirt. Looked like it either came straight out the washer, or straight off the floor. Probably the latter. He didn't strike her as someone who would clean anything. He wasn't married to the boys mum anymore. She died. Now he and the boy lived together, alone.

That was what the CPS was trying to put a case together with. Not much else on him. *Beats his kid.* Seventeen. Too old for social services to get involved. Old enough for the kid to move out. Why hadn't he? Misplaced loyalty? Fear, more likely. Gas-lit into thinking that whatever he'd done wrong was his own fault. *Take that beating.*

Amelia left the car and followed on foot. Hoodie, funnily enough. She'd dragged it off the passenger seat, on, hood up. A little warm in the city for it, but he'd made her face. Best keep incognito.

The evenings were drawing in. Wherever he was going, unless it was just down to the shop for a paper—not likely as he'd changed—it would probably dark before he got back. That suited her. Back to the hotel under cover of night.

And he was walking. So he couldn't be going far.

She followed him through a small park—along the river—to the high street. She kept her distance.

Darkness had fallen and she still hadn't finished that one pint of fucking stout. Other people must have thought her homeless. It was the only reason for her to still be nursing one fucking pint.

And those two were still talking horseshit about nothing. They were on to what a shit job Trucker had. He was a carer in a home apparently. Probably abused the old people. She should *probably* should stop calling him Trucker, but couldn't be bothered.

Finally the two of them stood. Dribbles still in their glasses. They'd had, what, four pints each. Usually one of them went for the next. Maybe they were finally leaving? They heaved themselves off towards the bar.

Amelia waited a couple of minutes for them to get in, and around. The pub was noticeably busier now. Young people. It was late afternoon, early evening. People were leaving work and coming in for a swift one before heading back home.

She followed them in. The two of them were up at the bar. Finishing the dregs of their pints. Waste not, want not, right? Amelia slid onto a seat next to the door. At a table with a couple of guys. Didn't pay them any attention.

She was still watching Trucker and Rogers.

"Drink?"

Amelia barely heard. A glance. She looked at

him. Then down at *their* table in front of her.

"You don't have one," he said.

No. She didn't. Fuck off. *I'm old enough to be your ... older sister.* "No," she muttered. "Thank you."

"You're welcome," he continued, unperturbed, or just wanted her to fuck off from their table but was too afraid to ask. "I just thought that you might be in here waiting for someone to ask."

Was he being rude? Hard to tell. The barman was looking at Rogers. He was frowning, but not saying anything. Something had happened and she missed it. Amelia looked around the bar. Over the other side. It was the two boys from earlier. They were still there. Rogers pointed at them. "Fucking bum bandits," he announced.

What the actual fuck?

Amelia was sure that she wasn't going to need more than that. He was a cunt, plain and simple, and was most certainly the sort to beat on his stepson.

"You should leave," said the barman. He wasn't particularly forceful either. Making the point to save face in front of the customers, but didn't really mean it. Rogers was a local. Regular. He was just mucking about. Had one too many. Doesn't really mean it. *That was how it went, wasn't it?*

Rogers and Trucker seemed to brush the whole thing aside, metaphorically, and started out the bar. People started talking again.

Fuck boy at the table with her was still saying something about buying her a drink.

Amelia shot him a look and stood. Shut him up. She went to the bar and the boys on the other side seemed to be having words now. It was like one of them wanted to drop it, forget about it, and the other wanted to follow the two of them outside and beat the shit out of them.

Well, they were only going to need to go after Trucker.

Amelia followed the Rogers and Trucker out the doors of the bar. Looked left. Right. They were gone. How? Jesus. She turned back towards Rogers house. Along the front of the pub. Reached the end of it.

Noise.

Down the alley at the side. Where they deliver beer. Surprised, she glanced.

Rogers and Trucker.

Waiting.

Fuckers were waiting for the boys to leave. *Shit.* What now? She couldn't just let them. They were clearly going to jump them and fuck them up. Two pissed up middle aged men, wanting to pick on a couple of guys having a nice night out. Well, it was nice before they opened their mouths.

Amelia reached the other side of the alley and out of view. She stopped. Think. She had to stop them. She pulled her hood down and returned to the mouth of the alley. Gave a look of light confusion, and then grinned. "You following me?"

C H A P T E R 1 0

"Oi, oi," Rogers blurted. "I remember you. What do you mean, following *you*?" He slapped Trucker on the chest with the back of his open hand. "This is my local."

Amelia smiled. She hadn't wanted it to go down this way. She was only supposed to be watching. This wasn't an opening to do her thing. This was *stupid* in fact. Fuck it. What was she doing? She'd just leapt into the jaws of the lion to stop it from taking a bite out of a couple of guys, both of whom might be fucking black belts for all she knew. The cascade of thought stopped her. She was aware that going too far down into the alley with these fuckwads might be a really—*really*—fucking bad idea. "I was just out," she said. "Wondered if I might bump into you."

He raised an eyebrow. Like this sort of shit never happened. It did happen. Just not to cunts like him. He *wasn't* attractive. He *wasn't* rich. He *was* obnoxious. He *was* trousered. Why on earth would anyone throw themselves at him?

Like, ever?

"Yeah?" he responded slowly.

Loser had no idea what to say. Flirting. Completely lost on him. Amelia sighed. She glanced over to the door of the pub as she stood in the mouth of the alley. A young woman came out. Staggered a little as the fresh air hit her, and then lit a cigarette.

"Yes." She unzipped the hoodie. Let it fall open. She wasn't in the mood for being seductive. It didn't come naturally.

She hoped she didn't have any Greggs sausage roll crumbs on her.

She knew that Trucker would fuck off if she could break the two of them up. Hoped the boys appreciated her efforts. "Walk?" she said to Rogers.

His grin became shit-eatin'. "Yeah," he said. Deeper voice. Hard to tell if he was taking the piss or not.

Trucker reached out, as Rogers seemed to be leaning in to start walking, unable to get his feet from the ground. He was far further gone than she was expecting. "We were doing something," he said. Tried to whisper. Failed.

Rogers shook his arm free. Snarled at the guy. Some sort of primordial signal that *man was on hunt for cunt*. Trucker did actually seem to get the message. He let him go. He backed into the alley, leaving Rogers with Amelia. She smiled at him. Sweet, like. He reached out and grabbed at her. Rough. The guy was a fucking animal. That was totally clear. He hung on to Amelia like his life depended on it.

If only he knew.

She leaned into it. Pretended she was enjoying it. The two of them leaving the alley and heading in the direction of Rogers house.

She glanced back but didn't see Trucker leaving.

But she was sure he would. He was probably just licking his wounds because his bestest buddy in the whole world had just left with a smelly girl. Fucking hell. She rested her head down on his shoulder as they walked. He would take it as some indication that she was heavily into him. But in reality, she was doing it so that he couldn't touch her face with his, see her eyes as he babbled on about what a great guy he was, or grab a handful of anything.

Shit. She was right in the middle of it now. Not much choice but to play along. After he'd made her in the car there was little cover left to blow. Now? None. It looked like she was making her own luck from there on in.

They turned the corner into the street he lived on. In the distance she could see the car. She *so* wanted to go and get in the car. Go back to the hotel.

Have a fucking shower.

This twat was such a mess. He stank. And not just from the beer. He had weird body odours. Well, body odour issues. His self-esteem must have been slightly larger than Mars, because he would not shut up about how fan-fucking-tastic he was at *everything*. And while the area wasn't cheap, as such, he did look to live in a bit of a hovel.

To the gate. Turned. In. The front door. He had his keys in his hand and was jabbing uselessly at the keyhole. Two sheets to the wind. Jesus. At least he should be more malleable like this.

She took his hand and guided it, holding the key,

into the lock.

"Looks like you're in charge," he said. Leered.

Fucker. The house smelt okay. Which surprised Amelia. She expected the fucking place to be a shit tip. Reek of week old curry. He tossed his keys noisily to the table on the inside of the front door. "Me casa," he said.

She wasn't sure what he meant. Maybe he'd seen too many films. "Indeed," she whispered, leaving his grasp and poking her head into the first room. Living room. Reasonable sized TV. Sofa. Beaten up, but serviceable. He was standing there, expectant. Looking at her. He was undressing her with his eyes. She didn't think that he would have the mental capacity to do it properly, and there was no way she was going to let him see the goods for real.

"Coming upstairs?" he asked, slurred.

Amelia shrugged. The man was a low-life piece of shit. Technically she didn't have enough to continue. Vic would look blank and say something like *We need evidence? Fuck that.* Which was pretty much how she felt about this guy. She looked past him to a family photo mounted on the wall. A woman. Him. And a boy. Maybe twelve. She nodded at it. "Your wife?"

Rogers turned. He took the photo from the wall. "Yeah," he said. Quiet. He stared at the picture. "The boy keeps it up." He placed the frame roughly to the table next to the keys. Let it drop face down. His eyes returned to Amelia. Her tits. "She's dead."

There is a look in the eyes of someone who has lost someone close to them. It's a fire—a spark—that appears every time their name comes up in conversation. It is the look of unsurpassed happiness as that memory, the face, the love … it's just *there*, for that second, as the memory of them overtakes the sadness of the loss. Then the sadness returns as the memory of death does. And the spark dies again, like it did when they found out the person was dead the first time. It's how you know if someone was truly touched by another. They die a little, with every happy memory.

Rogers didn't have it.

The memory of his wife was an inconvenience caused by a photo his stepson insisted went on the wall.

It meant there was no love there.

Amelia pursed her lips into the best smile she could. "And what's upstairs?" she asked.

"Then what did you come here for?" Anger bubbled under the surface of his words. He wasn't the sort of man—a term used loosely—who enjoyed not getting what he wanted. What he *expected*.

"Did you want to fuck?" she asked.

The grin returned. He concluded she was teasing him. Playing with him. She was going to fuck his brains out.

She wasn't. He didn't have any. Amelia pointed up the stairs. "Lead the way, handsome." Words that stuck in her throat. She just needed to be sure. It was *moral*. He started to stumble up the stairs, half pulling himself by the bannister.

Amelia stuck her head into the second door, behind the stairs as he climbed. Kitchen. Pristine. "Who does your cleaning?" she asked, returning to the bottom of the stairs.

"The boy," he replied. Belch. Loud one, too.

C H A P T E R   1 1

Rogers collapsed on the bed. He'd managed to unhook his belt and pull his zip down. Seemed to think that Amelia should do the rest. She pulled her hoodie off. He found that quite exhilarating judging by the noise he was making. She noted it smelt different in there, compared to the rest of the house. Everything out in the house smelt like … soap. In there … Amelia straddled across him. Put her hands on his chest. Leaning forward. Pushed her titties out. Get him going. Made him more compliant. He was saying things like *ooh, baby* and *you're so hot*. He wasn't *doing* anything, though. It was like he totally expected her to do all the work.

He was, as they say, though, *such a catch.*

She could feel him squirming underneath her. Like he was getting an—*shudder*—erection. Christ. "What can I tie you up with?" she asked suddenly. "I want to ride you like a chopper." *What the fuck? Shit, where did she get* that *from?*

He waved his hand to the chest of drawers pushed up against the wall. "In there. Ties."

She jumped off him and the bed, and pulled the drawer open. Suit ties. Sort of jammed in, in some ball, like an elastic band ball. She dragged the lot out, and unthreaded a couple as she went back to the bed. She took his hand and bound him to the bedpost. She'd had enough practice that she could bind him up like a prisoner of war. He grunted. She knew the knot hurt—his grunt, partly pain, partly pleasure. Fine. She did the other. Pulled his jeans open. Cock-waft freed, she screwed her face up a little. Fucker clearly didn't shower.

He noticed. "What's the matter, baby?" His words sort of mingled together when he spoke. *Whasama'er, baby?*

Fucking hell. "Hold that thought," she said. She put her finger to her lips. "And be quiet, if you want this when I get back." She slapped her arse.

He grunted and groaned and squirmed.

It all felt really … cheap.

Amelia left the room, pulling the door closed behind her but not latching it. In the hallway, again, the smell changed. It smelt nice out there. His bedroom, it smelt like dried up wank. Foul, pathetic little man.

Amelia walked along the hallway and pushed open the first door. Bathroom. Spotless. The boy—as *he* called him—did a cracking job of keeping the place clean. She went along to the next door. Pushed it open.

Fuck it.

The boy was sitting on his bed, staring at her. He was back from wherever he'd gone earlier in the day, staying in his room after the two of them had gotten back. "Oh," she mumbled, surprised. "Hi." When he'd gone out earlier she couldn't see his face. Now, she could see the bruising around his eyes. Across the bridge of his nose. Split lip. "Mel," she said. Stuck her hand out and walked into the room. Too late to hide herself now.

"Damon," he replied. He didn't stick his hand out, though. "You here with … Aaron?"

Amelia nodded. "Sort of." She glanced at the adjoining wall, between the room Rogers was tied up in and this one.

"Pretty thin. I know what you're thinking." Damon stood. "I'll leave you to it."

That was probably for the best. "What happened to your face?" She rested her hand on his arm as he went to pass her.

"Fell down the stairs." He shook her hand off and left the room.

That was all she needed. Amelia listened to him, going down the stairs, out the front door. Slammed.

"What's going on?" That was Rogers calling from the next room.

Amelia went to Damon's bed and rested down on it. There was a photo on the side table. Him and his mum. Roger's wasn't in it. There was another boy though. Looked about Damon's age. The two boys had their arms over each other's shoulders. Couldn't have been brothers.

She stared at the picture. It all made sense. Amelia stood. Out of Damon's bedroom, and to Roger's. Stuck her head in the door. He was struggling about. Wasn't sure if she'd left or not. "What's up, lover?" she said.

It seemed to calm him.

Back out into the hallway. Amelia tapped her finger on the bannister, looking over into the stairwell. Hmm. What to do with him. She wanted him to blurt it all out. Admit it. She went downstairs. Heard him calling after her. Excited. He wanted his *bite of the pie.* She wasn't exactly sure what that meant, but decided it was probably something to do with her body. The one he wasn't going to be seeing.

Into the kitchen. Amelia went to the knife block on the perfectly manicured counter top. She doubted that it needed much cleaning in there. Damon was unlikely to do much cooking—not if he was avoiding the place like he seemed to be—and the Neanderthal upstairs wasn't doing more than stuffing a pizza in the oven. Her finger rested on the cleaver, sticking up at the back of the block. Pondering. She wanted to use it to cut him up into little bits, but something was stopping her.

She hadn't thought it through.

She didn't have a change of clothes. No way of disposing of the body. Damon had seen her, although he didn't look *that* interested. He would probably be able to make her in a line up, but not get a decent enough portrait down at the nick for them to put this whore-cum-hooker together with Amelia Strange of Hellingate House. And she didn't have proof that he was guilty of much. But she *knew*. He had it written all over him.

She let her fingers drop from the cleaver to the bone shears at the front pf the block. They'd do.

CHAPTER 12

Rogers cock stood proud, just below his naked belly. Amelia had pulled his shirt open, the buttons flying free in the room. Pulled his boots off. His trousers. Let the obscure odour of his shitty hygiene roam nasally around the room. He was loving it.

She then straddled him. On his belly. So she didn't touch his cock. She didn't want to, and wasn't going to. She grinned down at him. He was starting to sober up now. He looked like he might blow at any second. One of the reasons she didn't want to touch him. She leaned in, forward, over him. "I saw the boy," she said, breathing hard. "Looks like you did a number on him. I like that. I like a *real* man."

Rogers grinned. "You ain't seen nothing yet." Vile pig of a man.

Amelia reached over the side of the bed and pulled the bone shears over his body. He froze. Still as the night. Not even breathing. She tapped the tip of the blades on his chest. His *dirty* chest. "Mmm." She moaned a little like she was enjoying it. She wasn't. And faking it was hard.

He breathed the word *what* out.

She smiled. "A real man," she whispered in reply. She opened the shears. Six inch blades. Sharp enough to get through the shin bone of a sheep. Hard enough not to chip doing it. She snapped them closed a couple of times. Open. Close. *Snip-snip*. Right between their faces. She did it so she could see his face. It—his face—dropped between strokes. She slid her arse back. Could sense his cock starting to droop too.

Fear.

She opened the blades back up. "What else have you done? I want to know. I want to know how much of a man you are before I fuck you." She grinned through the open blades. "You *do* want me to fuck you, right?" Wiggle of the arse. Felt his cock respond. This piece of shit was a *piece of work*.

"Yeah," he said. "What? What do you want to know?"

"Who else have you fucked up? In alleyways. With your trucker friend. What was his name?"

"Dave. Me and Dave have beat up on a lot people. Like to take out the trash. Cut down the weak."

The way he spoke. The glee in the back of his voice, he actually *believed* it. He thought he was some have-a-go hero, taking out the trash. Fuck a duck. "Who d'ya do?"

"Anyone   we   want.   Queers.   Homos. Sympathisers. Fucking insurance salesman."

Amelia bobbed her head to the side at the sound of the last one. He did have a poi—no. Focus. "You ever …" she paused, running the blades over his chest. The talk, it was exciting him more. She could feel him trying to hoick his hips around and rub his nob on her jeans. Fucking cheek. She pushed her hand into the front of her jeans. Shuddered. All lies of course. This was about as entertaining as watching The Great British Bake Off, you know, from a sexual point of view. Breathed in. Hard. Like she was getting off. "You ever kill anyone?" she asked. Kept her breath hard and her voice low. Pretence that the right answer might help her bring herself off.

"Yeah," he whispered. "I fucking killed."

She stared down at him. One hand on the shears. One hand in her jeans. "Who?" she asked.

Must have said it wrong. Rogers clammed up quicker than a chess player at a strip club. "Doesn't matter," he said. "Blow me. Blow me now."

He appeared to have bored with their little dalliance. Amelia pulled her hand from her jeans and took one of each of the handles of the shears. Pushed the open blades, sharp as obsidian, to his neck. Down enough to flex the skin inwards. A slit, thin as a paper cut under them. A trickle of blood.

"I knew," he said. "I knew there was something wrong with you."

"Who did you kill?"

Rogers didn't move. But didn't speak either. He wasn't playing. "Who are you?" he asked. Kept his throat still. The blades tight on his skin.

Amelia was a little impressed with how well he took it. She expected him to start blubbing, the pathetic human being, that he was. But he took the threat like a man. Huh. "Who did you *kill*?" she asked again. Pushed on the shears a little harder. Fucker actually smiled. But didn't respond. Amelia pulled the shears away from his neck. Left two tiny rivers of blood flowing slowing.

He seemed to relax, a little.

She slid the shears down his body. "Tell me."

"Fuck you. You don't have the fucking bottle. Untie me." He was *actually* trying to stare her down, as though she was some chav off the street.

It raised a little smile on her face. There was nothing she could do about it, of course, it just … slipped out. She pulled the shears open as far as they would go and moved quickly. Sharp. Over his left nipple. Slammed them shut.

Rogers screamed.

"Get used to it," she sneered.

Blood spat from the wound as his nipple bounced from his torso, landing wet side down on the sheets—already sticky from whatever God forbidden acts of carnal self-deprecation he'd belittled his own body with—with a sploop. A short fountain gushed upwards from the wound, a little like his tit had cum. Blood though. Then it steeped down to a slow river flow. All the while he thrust his body from side to side. It most probably hurt. "Diddums," Amelia said. "Who?"

Rogers realised that his legs weren't bound, and brought a knee up hard into Amelia's back. Pushing her forward, onto his chest. She stopped herself from plunging forward with the points of the shears pushing into his chest. The bone beneath.

"Cunt," he barked.

That was pretty much the straw that broke the camel's back.

Amelia slipped from the bed. She stood next to it. "Who?" she asked again. Didn't care if he was going to answer or not. He was flailing. Blood drooling out onto his filthy scabies-ridden torso, and he was rolling, flicking it back and forth. Onto the sheets. The walls even. Amelia had it on her shirt. She stepped forward, holding one of his legs down with a knee, and slipped the shear blades one either side of his testicle. The right one.

He stopped. Froze. Possibly shit too, judging by the smell, but it passed, so perhaps flatulence? "I'll tell you," he said. It sounded like he was going to cry.

"I don't care," Amelia replied. "Too late. Just going to assume you did your wife."

"I did." The noise came out like a wail. A child crying because he'd gotten caught with his hand in the biscuit tin. "*I killed my wife.*"

By this point Amelia couldn't care less if she had the words or not. She slammed the shears closed amputating the right testicle and some of the ball sack, too. The testicle, now detached did a funny little roll, emerging from the gloop within the scrote, out, onto his leg. Like a hard boiled egg. Amelia was a little surprised by how much blood gushed from the wound.

And how much Rogers screamed.

The house was a shithole inside, and pretty much

nestled up in the middle of a row of houses, all attached. Neighbours on both sides.

And Rogers was now making an unreasonable amount of noise. The sort of noise that gets you reported to the council. Civil disturbance noise.

She jammed the shears into his mouth, forcing his head still as he thrashed. She pushed. Snipped.

There was more screaming, although muffled because of the implements in his mouth. Like trying to scream when the dentist has his drill in there, along with at least two—sometimes three—hands.

Cut the tongue off. That should stop the screaming.

It did, but not how Amelia thought it should. She expected the lack of tongue to stop him making noise, but actually it was that he could no longer breathe, his mouth filling with blood. He'd swallow it back. Choking. Blood filling it again in seconds. He was literally drowning in his own blood, unable to stop himself because he was tied to the bed.

"Oh, you." Amelia said. "I'm not finished. How did you kill her?"

He stared at her, wild-eyed. Unable to respond. Couldn't speak. No tongue. Mouth filling with blood. He choked it out over his face. It made him look like he'd been skinned—

That was an idea.

—as tried to swallow it back.

"You swallow like a whore," she said. He was

making a noise like a cow giving birth. She took the shears, slick with his blood, and placed them around his pinky. Left hand. Pushed the blades together. Hard. Through the bone. And it was easier than expected, weirdly. He thrashed. His legs going everywhere. Blood spitting across the room from all the wounds.

Minor ones, *really*.

She cut off the next finger.

More thrashing.

"Weeeeeee." She grinned down at him. The thrashing seemed to be slowing. She wondered if he was tiring, or if it was blood loss. There did seem to be an awful lot of it around the room now. And he did seem to be lying in a pool of it.

She cut off his left testicle.

Again, it rolled off as if it were trying to escape the body. Over the leg. Down into the pooling blood on the sheets.

Plop.

She giggled. Looked down at herself as Rogers stopped moving. He'd managed to get blood pretty much everywhere. She wasn't too covered in blood to get home. Not like she was the final girl in a horror film or anything. Maybe she could grab one of the disgusting cunt's coats, just to get to the car. She should have moved the car back up the road while he was still tied up. *Before*. She smiled down on him and guessed he was probably pretty pale under there, but it was hard to tell, him having painted himself red.

The blood was slowly flowing from the wounds. His eyes were still open. There was a glint of life in there, but not much. He was getting tired. His body spasmed a couple of times. Death twitches.

"That's the blood leaving your muscles," she said. Dropped the shears onto his bare stomach. "It's all outside your body now." Smile. Warm. Leaning over his face. She looked deeply into his eyes. "You'll be on your way soon. My friend Vic tells me that you'll spend eternity in the warm embrace of excruciating pain." Rogers moved his lips. No words. Amelia leaned down a little. "You can't speak, remember? You can only breathe because there is so little blood left in your body—the heart isn't pumping much—so your mouth isn't filling with blood." She turned to the wardrobe and pulled it open. Musty. The smell of the room was of pennies. Old metal. It was the blood. She rummaged for a second like it was a rail of clothes in a charity shop.

Pulled out a raincoat. Dirty mac.

"Perfect," she said. She held it up. "You don't mind if I borrow this, do you?" Rogers didn't speak. Blacked out. Dead maybe. She wasn't going to check. There was no way he was getting up from that. She hung the raincoat over her arm and left the bedroom, closing the door behind her.

To the stairs and down.

C H A P T E R   1 3

Amelia got to the front door, dragged the coat on. Draped open. She pulled the door to the house open and stepped out, taking the two sides of the coat in her hand to wrap them around her.

Stopped in her tracks.

Trucker. *Dave*. He was standing in the middle of the path to the house, between her and the gate. Staring. Eyes wide. Amelia glanced down at herself. Blood. All over her clothes.

Then he ran at her. Some animalistic force took him. He was on her before she could move, pushing her back through the front door, into the house and over. She lost her footing on the doorframe. Hit the floor. It winded her. Amelia gasped for air. She'd landed flat, hard on her lower back. He was over her.

The front door slammed.

"What have you done?" he screamed into her face. Spittle and gob shone as it sprayed liberally from the man's gullet.

Amelia glanced side to side. *Fuck*. No weapon. Nothing. He stood over her. One leg either side of hers. *Kick him in the balls*. Then he drew his arm back. Fat fuck. She could barely see a defined body under the denim. He punched her in the face. Hard. Before she had a chance to do anything about it. The sheer weight of the blow. It knocked her head back onto the carpet. Bonked. Dazed. She saw flashes of white in her eyes. Tried to blink them away. Shit. Get it together. Before the fucker—

Another punch to the head.

Amelia lost the will to fight suddenly. Shit. This was it. He was going to stamp the life out of her. Her thoughts stopped racing. They became slow. Slugging about inside her head like she'd had fifteen Mules too many. She still had her eyes open, but she wasn't focussing on anything. Her face was numb. She could taste blood in her mouth.

Her vision, clearing, she realised that Trucker wasn't there. He'd … gotten off her. Gone looking for the source of the blood on her, she suspected. But she couldn't get up though. Couldn't move. It was like he had beaten the synapsis' that made her move, to shit. *No.* She wasn't finished. She was nowhere near fucking finished.

She'd barely started.

Amelia flopped a little. Tried to get up … normally. Get her body to do what her brain wanted it to. But that wasn't happening. She rolled around onto her stomach and pulled her knees up underneath her.

There was a scream. *Dave.* He must have found the body upstairs. He *sounded* like he had found God.

Amelia got to her knees. Up. Waved her hand out. It contacted with the bannister of the stairs. She used it to pull herself up to her feet. She could feel blood running down her face. When she reached up and touched her nose, her face went from numb to stinging like she'd been in the ring with Mohammed

Ali for a five rounds. Pulling her fingers away, she saw blood. Her blood. "Fucking hell," she muttered. She shouldn't have been caught off guard like that. She should have been able to take him.

Fucking, surprise, motherfucker.

Then she heard him. A weird growling fucking noise coming from the stairs … that she was standing at the bottom of. She looked up. Everything was still a bit of a blur. The guy had no fighting style, but he was big. Heavy. Fat.

And angry.

He was barrelling down the stairs towards her. Homophobic fuck. She ran. Into the kitchen. Stupid. She should have tried to get out the front door. Too late now. She pushed herself up against the counter and grabbed the cleaver from the block. Turned in time to see him coming at her. Fast for such a weeble looking cunt. Fist into her side. Missed the kidney shot. Still hurt. It knocked her off balance. She swung the cleaver as she tumbled to the side. Contact on Dave. It was enough for him to lurch backwards. But out of surprise and fear. The cleaver didn't break through the fucking shirt.

Fucking denim.

She slid along the counter. Eyes darting. She needed an exit as she wasn't in the right frame to fight this fucker. Not after he'd nearly knocked her head off. The back door. It was behind him. There was a table in the middle of the room. She backed around it. Luring him around after her. Playing a game of chase. She prayed that the door was open. Drew him around the table. She bolted to the door.

Fucking locked.

She nearly dropped the cleaver trying for it, too. Then the fucker was on her. Wrapping himself around her from behind like a motherfucking backpack. Pulled her up. Off her feet. Kicking out. She contacted with the back door, but didn't break the glass. The bear of a man was holding her up, arms wrapped around her, stopping her from moving. Dragging her back into the house.

She was fucked. She had no way of getting free.

C H A P T E R   1 4

Dave carried Amelia back into the hallway. Luckily for her, because of the way he was holding her, there was no way for him to actually *do* anything either. He was going to have to let go of her to even be able to hit her. And she was quicker than him, *right*? Trying to keep her wits about her, she waited for him to put her down. He seemed to be hugging her quite tightly, like he was trying to pull some bear-hug wrestling move.

It wasn't working, but she was hardly going to tell him that now. She still had the cleaver in her hand, too. Down by her side. Trapped.

He grunted some expletives as he put some energy into one final squeeze—that didn't do anything—then he let her drop to the floor.

She landed badly, skittered on her feet, and dropped to one knee, before she was up and turning. But she underestimated him. He lashed out at her. He couldn't actually fight for shit—bit of a brawler, maybe, beating on the helpless, no doubt—just like his friend, dead upstairs. He laid a blow to her shoulder. Bounced off. Then another swung in. She lowered the cleaver, hard and fast. Got it between the incoming fist and her own body.

Dave punched the blade.

It slipped through flesh far easier than denim. Cutting deeply in between the middle and ring finger knuckles. Slipped in betwixt the bone. An inch deep. Splitting his hand. He screamed out. Deep. A roar. And Amelia twisted the blade. The width of it made it easy. And twisting split the bone further. Fucked his hand. Blood exploded from the gash. Dave yanked his hand away to protect it.

Took the cleaver with it. Embedded in the flailing limb. Amelia didn't need to be told. She turned. Ran up the stairs. The only viable way forward. To the bedroom. Slammed the door. Back against it.

Fuck.

What was she doing? Now she was trapped in there with the corpse of Rogers. She was covered in his blood. If Dave called the police she was *actually* going to go down for it. Fuck. She heard him on the stairs. That was something. She pushed the door open. Ran at him. Screaming.

Flee. It was her only thought. If she could get away from the house clean, they'd never make her. Not in a line up. No way.

Dave looked surprised. He'd just gotten to the top of the stairs and had managed to pull the cleaver from his fucked hand. He was wielding it in the other hand. Starting to look woozy. Good. Amelia crashed into him before he had a chance to swing the thing at her. Not that he was that good at aiming—she hoped, at least.

The two of them looked at each other in the split second of them standing together, Amelia's momentum pushing them backwards.

Then Dave's legs gave, and they fell.

Further than they should have.

Over the top of the stairs. Onto the stairs. Tumbling. Pain. She could hear Dave crying out as the two of them tumbled over each other on the stairs. His weight on her. Off her. She was on top. Then him. There was a blade, somewhere. Stabbing pain in her arm. Twisting weird. Fuck.

Stopped.

Amelia wanted nothing more than to sleep, with something luring her to blackness. Her whole body was numb from the fall. She could taste blood. Her lungs hurt. Maybe it was her ribs. She tried to move her legs and her hips stabbed violently into her. At least her back wasn't broken. She moved her head to try and look around. Her neck wasn't broken either. She could feel Dave's mammoth fucking weight on her. He was lying across her. Still had the blade in his grip but he wasn't moving. Correction—he was breathing, but possibly unconscious.

The front door opened.

Damon.

He was standing there looking at her. Stood there for what felt like an eternity. Fuck. Bang to rights. Too fucked up to do anything about it. She was staring at him. Said nothing. What was there to say?

He pushed the door closed behind him. Didn't pull a phone or anything. Just sort of looked at her. "Aaron?" he asked, quietly.

Amelia tried to pull herself from under the dead weight, but her arm hurt too much for her manage it. "Upstairs," she said. "I … killed him. He deserved it." Still trying to pull herself out. She had to keep the boy talking and hope that Dave didn't wake up. She needed out. Now.

Too late to abort. Just run. Hide. *Hope.*

Damon walked over and touched Dave with his foot. "They both beat me," he said.

Amelia nodded. *Obviously.*

He came around behind her and put his hands under her arms. Pulled, saying, "You need to leave before he wakes up. Then I can say I just found him like this. I'll call the police."

Amelia's bones were on fire. It felt like she'd broken every bone in her body. "What about you?" she said. Little more than a whisper. Too fucked up to say more.

"I'll be fine," he said from behind her.

"Come with me," she said.

He snorted, pulling her legs from under Dave. "Go," he said. Dragged her up to her feet. He wasn't strong, but she was light.

She held onto the bannister. Taking her weight. "I can't leave you to do this on your own. I can protect you."

Damon shook his head. "You need to go. Now."

Amelia wobbled when she let go of the bannister.

He reached forward and steadied her. "I'm fine." She pulled the coat closed around her. Her face was still fucked up. Blood down it. No time for that though. "You're sure? Say now, or forever hold … you know? You'll never see me again."

"I hope not," he said. He looked down at Dave. He seemed to be coming too. "Go."

Amelia turned. Hurried through the door. To the street.

The car.

Safety.

C H A P T E R 1 5

The gates to Hellingate House opened and Amelia drove through. She hadn't bothered going back to the hotel. She'd just have her things forwarded. She would tell them that she had been called away for business.

It meant that she hadn't changed. Cleaned up. She didn't want to stop anywhere. She was a walking evidence folder. Hitting the driveway through the trees, she could see Cousins standing, waiting. Alerted by the gate at the edge of the property. *Shit*.

She pulled up, got out the car. It was hard to get out the car.

"Should I call for a doctor, Madam?"

She shook her head. Everything fucking hurt. The Mondeo had some baby wipes from KFC in the glove box. She'd used them to wipe her face while she was on the dual carriage way. But she was walking like she been fucked by a horse. Arm held up like it was in a sling. The coat flopped open as she stood. Cousins eyes dropped to her. She was covered in blood. "It's not mine," she said.

He raised an eyebrow, but didn't say anything. He was going to have to get used to this sort of thing. It happened surprisingly often.

She went into the house. The stairs. Back to her room. Amelia tore the clothes from her. Crossed her bedroom straight into the en-suite bathroom and turned the shower on. She looked herself in the mirror. Face was bloated. Bruising already coming out down her arm. On her shoulder. Hips. Fuck. She pulled the hair dye from the cabinet and set it on the sink. She might have to wait a couple of days to do that, for her body to be well enough.

———

When she got out the shower, returning to the bedroom, Vic was sitting on the bed. Human form. Naked. "What?" she asked.

"I was watching when you came home."

She shook her head. Strode to the drawers and opened them. Pulled out her knickers. A bra. "Always are, aren't you?"

He ignored the question. "You're not a goddamned superhero, you know. I've told you before." He stood. Came up behind her as she struggled to get her arms moving the right way to dress herself. He hooked the back of her bra.

Amelia turned and looked at him. In human form he was still far taller than she was. She dropped her eyes away.

"Who was it this time? Some runaway that you couldn't see like that? A young girl being touched inappropriately? Someone trusted … breaking the rules?"

She raised her eyes, meeting his. "Young man. His father was beating him for being gay. I couldn't stand by and watch."

"You know that none of these things will make a difference. It won't change the past, no matter how many times you try to put things right."

"I don't *try* to put things right. I *do* put things right."

"Murdering the guilty doesn't make a difference to you."

She turned, hobbling to the bed. Sat and managed to get her feet in the knickers.

"It won't change what happened to you," he said quietly.

"Shut up," she muttered. "It helps them. It makes me …"

"What? Feel better?" He snorted lightly. "And what about me?"

"What about you?"

"I'll do what you tell me to, no matter what. Forever. But I am far better served down there, than up here if you're belligerently going to vigilante around the country without me. What use am I sitting in the basement, playing with myself?"

She glanced to his cock. "It's still too large." Smiled.

Vic shook his head. "You're unbelievable."

Amelia stood. She went to the wardrobe and pulled out a dressing gown. Slipped it on. With difficulty. When she turned back into the room, he was gone. He was right, of course. It didn't put things right, and it *did* make her feel better.

Sending them to Hell. To the eternal damnation early. With a demon *she* raised.

And one day she would get vengeance.

For what happened to her.

CHAPTER 16

Amelia was sitting in the drawing room with a tablet, watching the live news on the BBC. Red head, now. She quite liked it, to be honest. Fiery. Made her feel strong and empowered.

Unlike her weak and battered body.

It had only been two days. She was still carrying two black eyes and interesting shades of brown and purple adorned large parts of her body. Vic had only made an appearance once since they fought, too. He was angry. Angry that she didn't just want him to eviscerate these fuckers. Sometimes she wanted to do it herself. She squinted at the images on the screen.

Some people she wanted to do herself.

David Collins. There were images of him being moved from one building to the next. Court houses. Collins … Trucker, sans beard. Wearing a suit. Very … respectable. *He'd found his best friend dead, and the killer, his stepson, all but standing over the body. Self-defence. That was why hospice carer Dave Collins has killed the boy.*

Lies.

And now Damon was dead. He should have come with her. Should have run like she did. But he wanted to face it. Fuck. Amelia tossed the tablet across the room, shattering it on the edge of a three hundred year old bookcase. *Shrug.* She buried her eyes in the heels of her palms. She could feel the sting as she did.

Stings that Rogers gave her. Stings that Collins gave her. Cunt.

She removed her hands. Blurred vision. She'd been pressing too hard.

Vic was standing there. Naked. Demon form. Made a change for him to be in demon form in the house. She looked by him to the door. Just in case Cousins was there. Then she looked back to him. Eyebrows went up.

"What is it?" he asked. His natural demon voice. Deep. Sounded like he'd had his throat cheese-gratered. She told him. He just stood and listened. The occasional nod. Coming over to the sofa, he sat next to her. He put his arm around her.

Amelia flopped into his arm as he held her. Buried her face into his charred flesh. Heat rising from the cracks in it. It was warming. Comforting, somehow. "I want him," she said quietly.

"I know."

Vic breathed deeply. The sound of Hell on his breath. For every gulp of air that went in, she could hear the faintest shrieks of thousands of tormented souls. Only when she was that close and it was silent in the room.

"I can fuck it all better," he said.

She slapped his bare chest.

He laughed. "If only the boys could see me now."

Amelia pulled back from him. "I'm serious. He fucking killed Damon. Out of fucking spite." She looked away. "Never once mentioned me."

"He was bettered by you, though, wasn't he? A strong woman. A weasel like that won't like that he was bettered by a mere woman. You know there was probably more between Rogers and Collins, right? That's what they say about those sort of people. Latent, I think they call it."

She snorted. "You're just trying to make me feel better," she said.

"Seriously," he protested. Hands out. *What?* He smiled. "So how do you want to do this?"

C H A P T E R   1 7

Amelia stood at the side of the road. In the darkness. Deep within the shadows. The roads between Ashbury and Canterford had no streetlights. One of the cars from the estate—a Vauxhall something—sat there on the side, hazard lights flashing. Bonnet up. It couldn't look any more like a trap. Not really.

Vic was standing, leaning against the bonnet. They'd bickered about how he should look. He wanted to go as an eighteen year old man. Short shorts. Tight t-shirt. Slicked back hair. Amelia argued that proving his point wasn't go to work, and Collins wasn't going to pull over for a guy. He might have been *latent*—the jury was still out on that one—but the jury in the ongoing court case was *literally* still out, and he wouldn't want to chance being seen. Not picking up a boy. She'd wanted Vic to look like a female whore. Short skirt. Looking dumb. Blond. That sort of thing. Fucking misogynistic wanker was sure to go for it. Fuck it—she'd have done it herself, if she thought he might not recognise her.

Vic relented, eventually. He also pointed out that if they were going to grab this guy in the middle of nowhere, he could just do it in his natural form.

But Amelia wanted him. All to herself.

Vic wasn't going to get to fuck this one. Not unless he wanted him afterwards.

Vic stood on the side of the road, Collins coming

over the hill in the distance. Rape fields on either side. Yellow, muddied by the late evening. He was on his way back home. One city to the next. Where they said he'd be. It was amazing how reliable information became when you could afford any demand without haggling.

Amelia pushed herself down, tightly behind the car. She could see it was his black four by four. He wasn't go to stop. Didn't drop his speed. Not a bit. Then he saw Vic. *She* was standing with her thumb out. Shorts. Very tight t-shirt. Amelia had told her her tits were too big, but Vic had insisted that she knew what men wanted better than she did, and if she was going girl, she was going girl *his* way.

The lights of Collins' car lit Vic up like a Christmas tree as he hurtled past, suddenly slamming on the brakes. He pretty much slid the car in, in front of the Vauxhall. Was out spryly. For a man of his size. Vic was right. Apparently the tits worked. Huh. Who knew all men were horn-dogs?

"What's the problem?" he called as he approached.

Amelia was more than aware that he was putting on a deeper voice. Fucking hell. *Men are such pigs.*

"I don't know," Vic replied. Weird high pitch voice he went with. She sounded like Betty fucking Boop. "It just kinda stopped."

Collins went to the car and looked at the engine. Shrugged. "Don't know much about cars. I can take you into Ashbury, though." He turned and faced her.

Staring at her chest. He wasn't even trying to hide it. "It's been a long day in court. I could use the company."

Fucking hell. He was in the fucking viewing gallery. It had only happened a couple of weeks ago. Preliminaries and everything. Made it sound like he was the fucking judge.

Amelia had enough of his horse shit. He was leering over Vic, doing little else, and Vic seemed to be enjoying it. Amelia shuddered. Weirdo.

She came out from behind the car. Collins didn't see. Didn't hear her approach. She had a syringe with horse tranquilisers in. Came from the stables at the house. She came up behind him. He heard then. Too late.

"Remember me?" she said, jabbing the needle into his neck.

Collins spun around to face her. Wide eyed. He looked surprised. A little scared.

"I told you," Vic said, gesturing down her body. "Tits."

Collins lifted his hands. Heavy. The amount of tranq was right. Practice makes perfect and all that. He spun in a little circle. Then dropped to the floor. Sprawled on the tarmac.

Vic was still gesturing.

"Can you get him in the car, please?" Amelia asked.

Vic nodded. She pulled the hulk of a man over

her shoulder. She carried him to the back of the Vauxhall and dumped him in the boot.

"Jump in." Amelia opened the driver's door.

Vic looked down at herself. Then over to Collins' car. "I don't know. I could head into the city. Get some action."

Amelia dropped her head to the side.

"Okay, okay." Vic opened the car and got in.

———

Collins was tied off on the pool table. He was spread eagle, one hand still in a cast from the cleaver incident. He was naked. Vic was naked too. Still a girl. Without clothing her breasts hung heavy, down onto her torso. Her mound was perfectly bald. As was the rest of her, from the neck down.

"He'll be coming around soon," she said. "I want to wake him up. Like a *lover*." She grinned at Amelia who was drinking a straight gin. It had been a long night.

Vic got up on the pool table and straddled across Collins chest. Legs spread. Right there in his face. "Wakey, wakey," she said. High pitched. *Betty Boop*. "Come on, lover, you were *soooooo* good." Jiggling.

Amelia shook her head.

"Come on honey bunny, baby wants some milk."

"You're not very good at this," said Amelia.

"Hush now," Vic snapped. She leaned forward. Rested her breasts almost on Collins chin. "There's enough here for a three-some."

As if he heard, Collins groaned. He was going to have a headache like the sun had exploded. The tranq did that to you. He pulled his eyes open. "What happened?" The words barely audible. Dry mouthed.

"You were amazing," Vic said. "Fucking and fucking and fucking. You were like an animal." She started to bounce as she spoke. Like Collins' bound body was a bull-ride. She squealed looking up to the ceiling. Playing with her tits like she was remembering.

Collins cock twitched.

He had no idea what was going on. No memory of the fictional events that Vic was talking about. He probably didn't even remember pulling the car over. But he was still getting excited.

Men.

Amelia was hidden behind Vic's body. Perfect view of Collins cock though.

"Yes," Vic said. His voice dropping a little mid sentence, like a hormonal teenager, voice breaking.

As his balls dropped.

Vic's skin started to burn first. The naked beauty of this late-teen-temptress flaring as the fire of Hell started to burn beneath. He put his hands up into his luscious head of hair and started to yank handfuls of it out with ease. His skull split open as horns grew towards the ceiling. His skin reddening. Blackening. All the while bouncing on Collins. Making orgasm noises.

Amelia couldn't help but smile. Vic certainly had a flare for the theatrical.

"Yes," he was saying. Over. And over. Deep voice now. Demon voice. His slender, sexy body started to flare out in places, bulging as he slowly changed from starlet to demon. Cracks appearing with lava flow beneath them.

His cock extending from where his cunt had been.

Growing out towards Collins' face.

Amelia circled the room to get a better view. Collins didn't notice her. He was staring at Vic, the face of an angel squaring. A hard jaw. Charred flesh.

"Don't forget," Amelia said over Vic's aroused noises. "He's mine."

Vic glanced at her. A smile. He knew. He was just playing. Vic's cock was fully out, squirming over Collins face like a viper, ready to strike, and Collins was slapping his head from side to side. Looked like he was trying to cry. He had his eyes firmly closed. Maybe thinking it was a nightmare, and he could wish it all away.

Vic started to grow. Getting harder. His arousal teased by the impending pain of David Collins. He gripped his cock. His huge demon hand sliding around it. "Oh," he said. Quick stroke. "Baby doesn't want to see," he said. He used his other hand to reach forward. Placed forefinger and middle finger onto Collins face, one finger just above each eye and pushed his eyelids up, holding his head in place at the same time. Started to stroke his demon cock right in the fuckers face. "You know what they'll do to you in Hell?"

Collins tried to shake his head. It was like he didn't want to know, *weirdly*.

Vic took a deep breath in through his nose. Sniffing. He looked Collins in the eyes. Collins eyes were transfixed on Vic's girth. "Impressive, isn't it?"

Vic actually nodded. *Nodded.*

Amelia came to Vic's side and slapped his shoulder. "Enough," she said.

Vic nodded, and started to get off. "He's pissed himself anyway."

Amelia looked around the brute size of Vic to the patch on the table between Collins' legs. Drooling out from him. "Oh," she said. "He's ruined the baize."

"I'll fix it later," Vic said. A hand went on Amelia's shoulder. "Do you want to be alone? You know how much I love to watch you work."

She shrugged. "I don't mind. You can stay if you want."

CHAPTER 18

Vic pulled a barstool into the corner of the room. Perched on it, barely fitting his bulk onto the small seat. Sat with his legs open, cock protruding.

Torture was definitely one of his *things*.

Scrub that. Most things seemed to turn Vic on.

Amelia leaned over Collins. Her face close to his. "Remember me?" she whispered. The sound of a female voice seemed to jar him from the sensory deprivation chamber he had created in his mind. His head flat on the pool table, he opened his eyes. Looked at her. The fat fucker was sweating. Blobs of it ran down his face. Into his thinning hairline. Disappearing from view. His eyes darted from side to side. Barely sitting on anything long enough to focus. He settled on Amelia. Stared at her for some time. She raised her eyebrows, questioningly.

Eventually he seemed to get the use of his frontal lobe back and nodded. Small nod. A little unsure.

"Good." She stood. Got further away from him. He smelt like piss. "Why did you kill Damon?"

"I don't know what you're talking about," he said quietly. He lifted his head. Saw Vic masturbating slowly in the corner. Made the noise: *Hhhrn*, and then dropped his head back to the pool table with a clonk. Bone on slate.

"I think you do. Admission will help relieve you of your sins—"

"No it won't," Vic interrupted.

Amelia shot him a disapproving look. "You beat me," she said. "You were unconscious when I left. *Why did you kill the boy?*" This fucker really got her goat. Normally she tried not to get too headstrong when she was only just beginning the process, but this … this … cunt, really ground her gears. He had his eyes shut again. Wishing it all away, no doubt. "I will cut your eyelids off, if you don't look at me when I'm talking to you." Scolding him like a child. Well. A child you're threatening with very real bodily damage.

He did open his eyes, though.

"I made Rogers tell me what he did to his wife before I let him bleed to death," Amelia continued. "You think you *won't* tell me your secrets."

"Keep that thing away from me," he hissed. His eyes gestured across towards Vic.

Amelia looked at him. He shrugged. Dropped off the stool. "You people are no fun," he said. Skulking across the room, he hit the stairs. Amelia could see him changing back to a human male form, dismissed to the upper floor.

For now, at least.

She looked back to Collins. "He's gone. Spill."

Collins shook his head. "You're going to hurt me."

"I'm going to do more than that to you," she replied. "It's just up to you how much it all hurts, really."

Collins took in a deep breath, then let it out slowly. "What do you want from me?"

"Are you fucking deaf?" she snapped. "Why did you kill the boy? How? They never said in the papers." She looked away, coy. "I didn't like to ask my contacts at Scotland Yard. Not with your pending disappearance." She looked back to him. "Why?"

"Fuck you." He snorted, rolled mucus around in his mouth. Then he spat it at her. It didn't get close. Dribbled and drooled from his mouth, most of it dropping onto his face.

"Gross," she said, rolling her nose up in distain. "Vic," she called. "You can come back in now. It appears that your presence doesn't matter one way or the other."

Vic returned. He was only waiting on the stairs.

Vic walked back across the room—in his demon form again before he got to the bar stool and took his place back on it. Erection in place. He started stroking again.

"Just gonna do that dry?" Amelia asked.

He spat in his palm, before continuing.

She giggled. Turned back to Collins. His face screwed up. "You look in pain," she said quietly. "I haven't even touched you yet." She looked down his gelatinous, flabby, sweaty, body.

"You'll pay for this."

The words were so strong, but said with such little power. He wanted someone to pay for this. He wanted it to stop. But it wasn't going to. And he knew it. Deep down. He was trapped somewhere. He didn't know how long he'd been there. No one knew he was missing. Amelia smiled, shaking her head.

"You'll go to Hell," he said.

"You first," she whispered. Amelia walked over to the side of the room and got the hostess trolley covered in tools. Instruments. She wheeled it over to the pool table. It squeaked as it wheeled like some demonic hamster wheel.

Eek. Eek.

Slowly to a stop.

Eeeeek.

She tapped on the top tray. "What to do," she mused. "You know, we try our best to make it, sort of, appropriate, you know? Some sort of ironic ending. Other times, not so much." She looked at Collins. "I don't know with you. Not so much I think." *Sigh.* "Thing is, you sort of needled me this time. Personally." Her eyes moved back to the trolley. "*Needled.*" She crouched and pulled a package of acupuncture needles from the lower tray. Tore it open. She looked down at Collins. "Hygiene first," she said, then laughed.

"What are you going to do?" he whispered.

Amelia looked at Vic. Winked. She pulled one needle from the pack and placed the rest of it down, back on the trolley.

Collins started to squirm. Really, squirm. "No," he said. "Please. Yeah, I killed the boy. What more do you want me to say?"

"Blimey," she said. "I haven't even started yet." She placed her hand gently on his forehead and took the needle. Lining it up with his eyeball. He closed his eyes. Started screaming. "Still haven't touched you." She spoke with the tone of a mother with a child, knee scraped, not wanting a plaster.

She pushed the point of the needle down, onto his eyelid. It slipped through the thin flesh. Into his eye beneath, nailing his eye closed. He could feel it. It probably felt really fucking weird, but acupuncture needles were designed not to hurt. She pushed it until it stopped, batting lightly against the bone at the back of the eye.

Collins opened his eyes. Eye. Whatever. He started to look around wildly. "What did you do?" he screamed. Spit firing from his mouth, landing on his sweaty body. "What?"

Amelia shrugged. "Heh," she said. It wasn't a real laugh, but she felt that he might take it as humiliation. And that was good.

Back to the table. A craft knife. Nice and sharp. "I think we should begin." That he wasn't in any pain yet was starting to bore her. She took the blade and showed Collins, over his good eye. She didn't speak. Just tilted it, so he could see what it was. Blade extended. She went to his arm. Pushed the sharp of the knife into his skin, right at the crease of the elbow. Not deep. Only a touch. Enough to cut through the skin, but not damage the nerve endings below. She wanted him to keep those, for now. Then she pulled the knife across his skin. Around the arm, circling it, so that she had broken the skin all the way around. So it wasn't attached now. It was a skin glove, elbow length. Putting the blade down, she fidgeted with the cut. Trying to get her fingers underneath. She wanted to pull the skin from his arm like the glove it was, now. But it wasn't budging. She jammed her fingers beneath the skin, unable to get a grip. Quick look to Vic.

Watching. He was stroking himself faster now. He nodded to her. "Keep it up." He looked down at himself. Grinned. "Yeah," he said, deeply.

Amelia turned her attention back to screaming Collins. She'd managed to loose blood from his arm. She could see the flesh beneath, but the skin was attached. "Fuck it," she said. For whatever reason she really wanted this, now. She scooped the blade back up and started to flick the edge around the flesh that was held to the skin. She just expected it to be like putting butter under a chicken skin—something she'd helped the housekeeper do *once* when she was a child. Fucking disgusting. But it was more attached than that. Jab. Slice. With each hack of the blade, more of the skin came away, blood stopping her from seeing what she was doing. It was pooling out onto the table beneath him. *Pool table*, she thought. *Ha*.

He was still screaming.

"Ugh," she blurted at him. "Shut up will you." She stopped. Stabbed the knife into his moob like a chef into a chopping board at the end of an episode of some fucking cookery show she was too drunk to change the channel from. She looked around the floor. Grabbed his underpants. At least they were clean. She jammed them in his mouth. Pulled the blade back out. He seemed to be more half crying and screaming, than just screaming now. She'd gotten his glove some four inches from the elbow. "Should there be this much blood?" she asked.

Vic made a growling noise. Something *horny*. Then said, "You probably hit a major vein. Hm?"

Hm, indeed. She picked up Collins shirt from the floor and started to wipe the blood away. Every time she pushed it off his flesh, more appeared. "You might be right."

"Here," Vic said getting up from the bar stool. "Let me see." He walked over to the pool table. Cum on his hand. He wiped it over Collins—who was thrashing from side to side as best he could. He looked at his arm. Poked it really hard.

Collins screamed through his pants.

"Yeah. Broken a vein. Dude's gonna bleed out pretty quick. If you want to hurt him, then you should probably get on with it."

"Can't you do something to stop it, *demon*?"

Vic scowled at her. "I could. But I'm not really in the business of stopping people from dying. *Capiche*?" He even fauxed up an Italian accent.

"Shit."

Vic returned to the stool. Still hard. Started stroking again. "Anyway," he said. "You won't learn if I always help you."

Amelia shook her head. "Right," she snapped. Pain. She needed to cause pain. She dropped the craft knife to the table. Too small. Too slow. She picked up a Black and Decker battery powered drill. Had a wood drill in it. A wide one. She pulled the trigger, spinning the chuck up. "Yes," she said. "*Yes*."

Amelia pushed the spinning drill bit into Collins side. About halfway down his torso. He screamed again, managing to push the pants from his mouth. Some of the flesh wrapped around the drill bit, travelling up it like an electric whisk, and bread dough, tearing from his body, slopping to the floor. Made some *Nooo* sound, that may or may not have been an actual word. Then he managed to contort his face so much he opened both his eyes, snapping the acupuncture needle in half, half in his eye, half protruding from the lid.

Amelia pulled the drill out, and then pushed it in again, a little higher. Felt it bounce off the bone.

"I did it," Collins was mumbling amidst the screams. Probably felt half asleep through blood loss. "I killed the little cunt. I beat his head in."

Amelia pulled the drill out. She must have hit something after slipping past the ribs, because blood jettisoned from the wound. "Why?"

"He's a fucking queero," he said, but quiet. Starting to slipping away.

"He's dying," said Vic.

"Good," Amelia said. Nodding. She jammed the drill in again. Down the body some, in the ripped whole from the first push in. She whirled it around a little like she was trying to make a hole bigger. She sneered into his face. "You smelly fucking cunt-bag," she said. "You'll spend all eternity being fucked by demons, raped, the skin flayed from you." She pulled the drill out and tossed it to the table. Then she punched him on the nose. It made her feel better. "God forsaken rat-faced, bucket of smashed crabs." His insides had been drilled through. Some of his guts still hanging off the end of the drill bit. The hole in his side was huge, blood drooling from the edges.

Collins moved weakly.

Death at his door. Knocking.

"I wish I could do more," Amelia said, quietly. "It doesn't seem like enough."

"This one got to you, didn't it?"

She nodded, turning into Vic's arms, as he put them around her. "Would you like to set fire to him?" he asked, soothing, seductively.

Amelia felt tears welling in her eyes. "Can I?"

Vic pulled her from his warm—burning—embrace and looked down on her. "You get the accelerant, I'll get a fire extinguisher."

Amelia hurried behind the bar and pulled out the Spirytus Vodka while Vic went to the stairs and got the fire extinguisher from behind them.

Collins was moaning, barely conscious. Pain from his eye, his side. But he deserved more. He moaned out as Amelia splashed the high alcohol content spirit over him, freely, then she looked to Vic. He was standing with the extinguisher at Collins head.

Amelia pulled a lighter from the trolley and lit him.

He shrieked out, a sudden volume neither Amelia nor Vic expected him still to have, as the basement filled with the stench of burning human flesh. Fire raked over his body. The scream stopped when the fire reached his face. In his mouth. His throat. Cooking him from the inside out. He stopped moving, and Vic fired the foam over him. Putting out the flame.

Sizzling coming from under the white foam, Collins smelt a little like fucked up barbecue. There was a strange gurgling sound. Then he shit. It ran out onto the table. Purging in death. The shit steamed out in the midst of the foam. Hot.

"Fucking hell," Amelia said, waving her hand in front of her face.

"Better?" Vic asked, smiling.

CHAPTER 20

Amelia was sitting at her desk in the office. Vic, human form, sitting opposite. "You could wear some clothes."

Vic looked down at himself. "Cousins is out. It's only courtesy that I've bothered to change at all."

"That, and you wouldn't fit in the chair otherwise."

Vic ran his fingers down the arms. "True. When are you going to get furniture designed for the real man?"

She smiled. Lifting the brown envelope in front of her—the one she'd been going through while they chatted—for him to see. "We have a job."

"What is it this time?"

"It's a woman."

"Unusual," he replied, eyebrow raised. "Go on."

"Seems to think herself a femme-fatale. Picking up men, having her way with them and leaving them for dead in hotel rooms."

Vic lifted his cock—too big, but flaccid, at least—with his left hand. "Does that mean you need me to …?" He grinned like a child on Christmas morning.

Amelia nodded. "Yes," she said. "You'll need to bait this one."

About the Author

Ash is a British horror author. He resides in the south, in the Garden of England. He writes horror that is sometimes fantastical, sometimes grounded, but always deeply graphic, and black with humour.

Printed in Great Britain
by Amazon

18593262R00058